PRAISE F[...]

"... a timely critique of the relationship between the human emotions underpinning the desire to create, and the increasing automation of the creative arts. Sharp, pointed, and prescient."

- ISABEL J. KIM, SHIRLEY JACKSON AWARD-
WINNING AUTHOR

"I AM AI is a brilliant tale of humanity in a heartless corporate dystopia, where friendship and found family offer some respite from ruthless capitalism and divisive commercialism... that embraces such diverse characters of colour and queerness.... an emotional journey simultaneously universal, and grounded in the Asian experience, down to the all-healing, magical power of soup."

- XUETING C. NI, AUTHOR OF SINOPTICON: A
CELEBRATION OF CHINESE SCIENCE FICTION

". . . an unflinching science fiction masterpiece that's essential reading to understand where today's world could be heading."

- JASON SANFORD, AUTHOR OF PLAGUE BIRDS AND FINALIST FOR THE NEBULA AND PHILIP K. DICK AWARDS

". . . I AM AI takes the seeds of increasingly tech-enabled late stage capitalism that currently pervade our world and extrapolates them. . . . Ai Jiang reminds us of our own hearts, and of the things that matter most, the things that make our hearts sing."

- WOLE TALABI, LOCUS AND NEBULA AWARD NOMINATED AUTHOR OF SHIGIDI AND THE BRASS HEAD OF OBALUFON

"I AM AI is a terrifying, prescient, and prophetic story set in an alarming future that, if we're not extremely careful, might be lurking right around the corner. It's required reading for every human being that cares about art, writing, love, family and the creative life that makes us human."

- KAREN OSBORNE, AUTHOR OF ARCHITECTS OF MEMORY

"I AM AI is a tense, lean narrative that thuds along like the compulsive, essential beat of one's heart. Jiang has something to tell us in this story beset by a dystopian future where the boundaries between real and artificial are blurred: to strive is to be human, and therefore we must cling tight to wanting."

- EM X. LIU, AUTHOR OF THE DEATH I GAVE HIM

"Ai Jiang is a master at using SF to shine a light on the dangers of our present moment. I AM AI is a rich, cautionary tale with the power of fable."

- RAY NAYLER, AUTHOR OF THE MOUNTAIN IN THE SEA

I AM AI

I AM AI

A NOVELETTE

AI JIANG

Shortwave Publishing
contact@shortwavepublishing.com
Full Catalog: shortwavepublishing.com

I AM AI is a work of fiction. The characters, incidents, and dialogue are creations of the author's imagination or are used fictitiously. Any resemblance to actual events or persons, living or dead, or events is entirely coincidental.

Copyright © 2023 by Ai Jiang

All rights reserved.

Cover design by Chun Yan Zhang, Ai Jiang, and Alan Lastufka.
Interior layout by Alan Lastufka.

First Edition published June 2023.

10 9 8 7 6 5 4 3 2 1

ISBN 978-1-959565-09-3 (paperback)
ISBN 978-1-959565-10-9 (ebook)

*To those who believe they are never enough:
you are more than enough.*

I AM AI_

It's becoming difficult and dangerous to ignore my battery's rapid run-down time. At 8%, my memory functions are diminishing far too quickly. I've forgotten to charge before leaving work —again.

For me, forgetting is a dangerous thing.

I hope the glitches don't cause a sudden short-circuiting.

The notification for my postponed-for-half-a-year maintenance glares from the watch implanted into my wrist. I press snooze, my fingers trembling. I can't afford the bi-monthly checkups, but I'll need to replace my battery soon.

Replacing my brain for a system that works faster, that limits errors, and doesn't cause memory gaps becomes more appealing with each passing day. AIs don't have a fear of overworking, of needing sleep to prevent any fatigue.

My hands shake at the prospect of finally getting rid of the one thing outside of my brain that hinders my productivity. To think my emotions will soon become a muted thing, I can't tell if I'm afraid or eager. But I'll be able to work faster. Joy and pain won't affect me in the same way.

None of my neighbours know I die with my battery rather than my heart. Most of them still believe I'm more human than robot—half metal and circuits. Being less human makes life easier. Technology is convenient; it's more dependable as a life force, more predictable. Emotions, humanity, mortality; humans are such fragile things.

A message from my mechanic Joan arrives, pinging my watch with an "URGENT" tag. *I've secured the battery you've been looking for to make the full heart replacement. You're booked for tomorrow.*

I appreciate their straightforward tone, though a part of me wants us to become friends, given how long we've known each other. Three years now, maybe four—I've lost track. But I suppose it will only become a nuisance to us both, draw us away from our focus, if we care too much.

I just have to hold on until tomorrow night.

Another warning about my battery. I dismiss it and scramble to leave, grabbing my jacket flung in the corner of my 11 ft. by 11 ft. box-like unit, to reach a charging port on time.

I don't notice Auntie Narwani's entrance until she's long pushed her way into my unit's narrow space. I almost curse out loud as I mentally make a note to fix the lock.

Auntie Narwani hovers by my elbow, trying to plug the clock she found last week into the port in my arm. I should be annoyed, but the feeling of familiarity, the sense of family she has somehow built in our community over time, even if we have no blood relation, comforts me. Sometimes I want nothing more than to collapse into Auntie Narwani, but to show such weakness will only create bad, *time-costing*, habits I can't afford.

Right now, I don't have the patience or battery life to entertain the elder's requests. Cold sweat wells at the base of my neck, collecting in the collar of my shirt, long due for a wash. Grime itches the parts of my back that remain skin rather than metal. I can almost hear my battery draining within me as the seconds tick past.

"Hold on a second, just hold on *a second*!"

I don't have a second.

Our arms flail, and I narrowly miss her head at the same time she accidently sucker punches my shoulder. Cold air whisks down my lungs. I add "shoulder-plate" to the list of replacements I will purchase when funds allow.

She plugs the clock back in.

The clock is precious to Auntie, but to me, it only serves as a reminder of the time I'm losing, the stutters of my heart when the passing minutes appear as a looming count down within my mind.

The old thing had washed ashore, waterlogged, paint half gone, with the seconds hand missing. A great find, she explained, even though she'd cut herself on the jagged edges of rocks and soiled her shoes trying to reach it by the edge of the lake. It never lasts long enough for the alarm to go off at the time she's set it for. Sometimes, I feel like the clock. My energy levels and brain capacity always coming to a halt when I need the limitations removed most; the choking suffocation of imminent burnout a faceless entity chasing me from behind with shadowy fingers always just brushing the small of my back.

I keep reminding her to toss it, to get a new watch—one that tells time without stuttering. But she never has. The protective coating of the broken clock's wire is barely there, like flesh hanging from exposed bones. If unlucky, we both could be electrocuted.

Look at how wonderful it is, Auntie Narwani insisted. *There is a story behind this clock.*

"Auntie!" I swat her hand away once more, impulsively checking my battery again and again, with each staccato movement.

Just because I'm a cyborg, she sees me as both an endearing youth and a tool for her use—but sometimes it feels as though the latter is truer than the former. Here in the city of Emit, we're more valuable as tools than humans.

"Hush, child," she says, frowning, looking at me as if *I'm* the one in the wrong.

I don't want her to know she is leaving me on the verge of death.

My palms clam up, sweat beads at my forehead as I look for a way to leave without being rude. Guilt claws at me when Auntie Narwani makes a disappointed pout. She acts more like she's seven rather than seventy. I wish to be as carefree as she.

The light above us flickers. Outside, the rest of the units' electricity goes out. I check my Bluetooth connection that helps power all the other units. Disconnected. My aid all started as a way to make some extra cash on the side, but over time somehow just became a favour I did for everyone. Whether it's compassion or guilt or pity, I much prefer to see everyone sharing what little resources we have, rather than hoarding everything myself.

Electricity is a luxury we can barely afford on the outskirts of Emit. These shelters were not built by the government, but by those who couldn't afford the property rent in the city. But they still charge us.

A few of our neighbours peek out of their units. Some climb onto the intricate metal staircases that connect our honeycomb-like community under the bridge that stretches from the mouth of the city Emit, across the lake, leading into barren, infertile land. Many of us prefer it to the bustling noises of the city.

With the city's overpopulation, they've begun building homes and shelters wherever there is space—digging underground, growing upward, or, like our homes, under the bridge, attached to its legs. There used to be houseboats floating across the lake, until New Era's monopoly over all industries. They claimed the body of water as their own and complained about floating bodies and debris after heavy storms. They don't care about the dead, only the cost of fishing the corpses out, and the resources to return them to their family. To New Era, people might as well be the plastic bottles floating in the lakes—before those bio-engineered to consume garbage in efforts to clear the growing landfills began risking their lives to fish them out of the water. Roaches. I wonder what names they might give people like me.

A thundering of steps echoes towards my unit. It was no doubt Nemo making her way in a zigzag up the three flights separating our homes.

I check my battery again.

7%.

"Ai?" The young child pops her head in. Normally her mother Lei stops her from visiting too frequently, but the young child latched onto me as though I'm her older sister ever since her mother began taking on extra shifts at work.

Nemo pulls out her drone controller—a small thing the community pooled together to buy her—and lands the machine by her feet. From its body, a hologram pops up. A shining gold coin displays what I'll need to pay the government this month. Then, it switches to a hovering diamond that holds the remaining debt I owe the government.

I nudge past Nemo and swallow the hurt expression that warps her joyous face and leave Auntie Narwani still cross-legged on my bare futon.

In the distance above us, at the end of the bridge that divides the tech-drenched city and our honeycomb home, Emit's glow is unwavering. Its skyscrapers claw into the clouds, the tops unseen

—a city that progresses and moves at a speed too fast for many of our minds. Most of the others refuse to pay for the upgrades, desiring to remain more human—not me. Being human reminds me of my parents and the fragility of our minds and bodies, the way New Era drained their life's hourglass, among other workers, at double speed. No doubt their worries about leaving me with my aunt as a child accelerated their burnout. I cannot afford the same.

"Leaving for work again?" Auntie Narwani fidgets with the clock. Why she always sets it for 5:00 p.m., I'll never know; I'm never home until 10:30 p.m.—at least.

"Yes," I say in a rush, focusing on the beckoning allure of my watch.

Still 7%. But it won't remain the same for long.

Before, it might take up to half an hour just to drain 1%.

I often wish I could live simply like Aunt Narwani and the others, thriving on what they grow near the bank along the lake, away from the prying eyes of the Emit government, taking up odd jobs when available. But I can't; none of it pays enough, nor are the hours consistent—not anymore.

I think of Auntie Narwani and how she might spend the day. Sometimes she mentions cleaning for the New Era towers, or the barely lived-in homes of some techies, offering her services for cheaper than what they would pay machines. But what makes her services unique is the songs she sings, the shaking notes, the occasionally off-pitch tunes, that fill the towers and homes with something other than the hum of electricity—a voice I sometimes catch as I drift to sleep each night. She makes just enough to get by and has no desire to climb any social or economic ladder. After being replaced by music machines and bots at the karaoke hubs and scattered bars when they first appeared, her only desire is to sing for those who might appreciate "real music".

I used to want the same; for someone to simply appreciate the stories I write, even if flawed, with loopholes, inconsistent characters, endings and openings barely hanging on like threads. But when my parents passed, all they left me was their endless debt and memories that bombard my mind at night. I see the hardships my parents went through as techies for New Era, images of their early passing, being shuttled out of New Era's main tower—Father only thirty at the time, Mother, twenty-nine, and I was only seven.

I still have vivid dreams of the many deaths that day, the injustices when New Era offered the families of the dead nothing but a written letter of insincere apology, and the protestors. Almost as soon as they gathered, their efforts were suppressed by New Era security. Protests are rare now, if any. If I could wipe myself of these memories, I would. The holographic ads hovering above the New Era-owned buildings in Emit come to mind: *Brain replacements are the best option for the tired mind!* Then again, which buildings are *not* owned by New Era.

They offered me a job too, New Era, but I still haven't taken them up on their offer. Even after years of blistering skin, the shiver of rising goosebumps tightening, contracting across my limbs in the middle of the cold of the dead season, on the verge of hypothermia, I still refused.

My work isn't so different from New Era and pays far less. But it isn't *as* mindless and repetitive. There is always the pressure to be perfect, to limit errors, to the level of AI—0.001% or is it 0.0001% now? But limiting errors also means taking away style, and the systems aren't as good with coming up with anything unique and often draw on what already exists and the cliches. Most are content with the creative texts AIs produce, though there are still those who prefer more "authentic" voices, yet almost none of those people are willing to pay the price.

Some large corporations might seek out people like me once in a while, when they're looking for something *"Fresh! Never before seen!"* Contrary to what they hoped, not as many artists and writers jump at the chance to work for them. Some do, but it can be such soulless and tightly controlled work.

6%.

"Don't be home too late!" Auntie Narwani calls after me as I speed out of my unit and up the steps. I try not to look down. I listen for incoming traffic, even though there is almost always none, before pulling myself over the side railing and onto the bridge's asphalt surface.

Later at night, I'll have to charge Auntie Narwani's clock again and power the reading lights and night lights for the elderly and children, hot water for Mrs. Gem, who finds relief for her pregnant belly while standing for fifteen minutes under a warm shower. There is a couple who always has something broken, and the sound of their electric drill buzzes for an hour or two upon my return. And of course, Nemo, who always comes running to charge her drone because, outside of delivering any news from Emit, she wants to watch the sleepless city, even if she can't live within it.

The path towards Emit is worn, cracked under harsh rays of sun. The city avoids making repairs to the bridge whenever they can. Few people cross it by crafts or e-bikes anyhow, and when they do, they usually never return.

I check the time—

5%.

With Auntie Narwani's insistence this morning, I'm already a few minutes behind for work. I can't lose any clients.

A light drizzle begins that quickly pours.

Rain isn't nearly as harmless as it was before: the droplets are corrosive to both skin and metal, skyrocketing the prices of waterproof parts. I can't afford any of those expensive replacements either, though I suppose with how often I have to change my parts, it must have added up to the same cost anyhow. I pull out my compressed raincoat, unfurl it, and toss it on. Droplets eat away at the material that remains and at the mixture of skin and metal of my limbs peeking through the holes.

I work up to a slow jog, cautious of how heavily I'm breathing, in hopes I'm still alive when I reach Mao Tou Ying internet café.

I suppose it wouldn't be too bad if I passed,

though I dread to think who might end up with my debt. Unfortunately, New Era didn't care about those with no families. They can easily pass debt onto someone they think we might be close to, who their cameras might have spotted us with. Knowing this, I fear they might go for Nemo.

I can't tell if what burns down my cheeks is rain or tears, but I suppose it doesn't matter because one eats from the outside and the other within.

4%.

MAO TOU YING sits at the edge of Emit, just far enough to not garner too much interest from the government, but close enough it can reap the benefits of the city's electricity sources and communication infrastructure. Like many of the Independents, these owners and companies are pushed to the edges of Emit, as far from the city center as possible. It wasn't their choice, but I think if they had one, they would still choose to remain in place.

Atop the entrance of the café are the flickering neon aqua letters of Mao Tou Ying and the wired image of an orange owl sitting on top of "Tou" as though perched on a tree, the wavering colour making it seem like it's on fire. Sometimes only the "Ying" is lit, and without the tonal accent, no one can tell whether it is the "ying" in owl or the "ying" in shadow. Ironically, both fit the establishment.

I pick at my peeling, exposed skin and at the buildup of rust on metal and wince, regretting replacing only the areas around my joints rather than the entirety of each limb. I thought about replacing my hand so there would be no finger fatigue, but I didn't want to give up the feeling of the keys against flesh. Somehow, that makes the act of creation feel more real, tangible.

Smoke wafts upward just past the café where a street vendor, Nemo's mother Lei, lives with the rest of us under the bridge. She stands at her stall stir-frying freeze-dried rice after defrosting it with a drop of New H2O.

Lei spots me and beckons me over.

I shake my head quick.

3%.

"Maybe after work," I call out and smile, but it falters at the age lines on her face that seem to deepen by several folds each day.

Lei insists on working most of her hours away. *The baby's almost three, and New Era raised tuition for preschool again,* she'd explained a week prior. People believed New Era would soon collapse after its initial rise because of the increasing burnout rate and decreasing life-expectancy of their staff. But the company managed to strike a balance after branching out to take over other industries. Emit's average life expectancy is up from forty-five to fifty years—but that is nothing compared to our ancestors a thousand years ago, in 2022, when life expectancy hovered around eighty.

Lei always begins work far before the sun starts to rise, hiding behind the smog-infested skies, and much after it sets, when the only light in this alleyway comes from the fire of her wok, the glow-in-the-dark painted sign of her stall.

I pull up my e-wallet and search for the name of her stall, Fried Wok Street Food—easy for tourists to find. The order option pops up after I tap the holographic name, and below it is the option to tip. I don't have much extra to spare, but I send two Coin—half the price of a rice bowl, knowing that even if I don't end up buying dinner, Lei will bring home leftovers and leave them by my door anyhow.

I'm wasting precious seconds. I know. Yet I find myself unable to escape this daily ritual, no matter how dire the circumstances. It feels as though it is one of the only small intimacies left in my life.

Lei shakes her head, but a grateful smile rests on her lips. She swipes a perspiring arm, tanned up to where her shirtsleeve covers, across the white bandana that encases her forehead. Though I need every Coin I can get, I can work longer hours, accept new clients to make up the slight loss. Lei will need it more than I do. She reminds me of my mother, who was always working when I was a child. Back then, I couldn't understand why she spent so little time with me, but now that she's gone. . . I hope Nemo won't grow up misunderstanding Lei, but I know she probably will.

2%.

I buzz Wushui to let me in. Wushui turns off the screen-frosting security function on both the glass of the door and windows, even though he already has cameras installed outside. Maybe the cameras are broken. There is always something broken in the café, but luckily the e-glass screens —floating digitalized glass that resembles a more minimalist version of old computer monitors— are not one of those things.

I glare into Mao Tou Ying while I wait, unamused at his usual lack of urgency.

Still 2%.

It's packed today, with the regulars, teens, playing video games in a corner or live streaming in one of the six booths in the back. From the looks of it, half of them use scripts written by New Era's A.I. app. One of the booths has been blacked out since Hermes, a neighbour who reminds me of myself sometimes—a girl I barely see in her unit—booked out the booth so she can paint with what little supplies she can afford and get her hands on. She occasionally keeps her finished works, and I would see small pieces hanging on the otherwise bare walls of her unit, or the communal washroom at the center of our honeycomb; other times she might sell them to black market collectors or to New Era.

Some of the customers are masked, some unmasked. I always wonder if they worry about their identities being exposed, but everyone at the café is usually too absorbed with their own thing to worry about anyone else. One thing Wushui requires us to do is wear noise-cancelling headphones. But with some regulars, he's grown lax.

1%.

Agitation swims at my temples in throbbing waves, and I raise a fist to pound. But before my knuckles meet the door, there is a click. I push my way inside, shivering from the walk in the rain.

"Hey, Ai, you know the rules," Wushui grunts as I'm about to leave the muddy, rubber floor mat and step onto his precious royal blue carpet.

Wushui—*No Sleep*—isn't his real name, but a

nickname that has become part of his identity because his business never closes, and he never seems to go home. He's long since become jaded and no longer seems to care about whether or not his business fails. He spends most of his time reading digital magazines and newspapers that are too old, outdated—always subscribing only for a month before cancelling, downloading all the content he can before the subscription ends.

I flash him the whites of my eyes before kicking off my boots, then hold up a foot, wiggling the toes inside my damp socks.

Wushui's partner flits out from the back room and makes a beeline towards me, swatting at my foot, though only half-heartedly, and offers me his usual lecture on respect. Niao, true to his name, is bird-like and gentle and, of the two older men, slightly more energetic. He's always making coffee and offering water to customers, trying to make sure people don't pass out too often while they're in the café. They do anyhow, but the kind gesture is appreciated, except by those who seem too immersed in their work to notice. At the end of the day, much of the water and snacks Niao leaves by the e-glasses remains untouched.

Wushui offers an almost unnoticeable breathy laugh without looking up from the handheld e-glass screen in front of him, likely reading the news about recent electricity outages with silent judgement.

I dip low and collect my boots, throwing them on the rack next to everyone else's shoes. There is one pair of slippers, oversized, that I always like to wear best. And though Wushui and Niao never make it explicit, they always leave them on the side for me; Niao even put a small sign beside them, warding off other customers. I thrust my feet into the slippers.

Please connect to a power source—

I try not to show my growing nervousness as I speed walk to my seat, connecting the wire extending from the e-glass into my charging port. An audible exhale whistles through my nose at the sight of the small lightning bolt blinking on my forearm.

There is a laugh paired with an unfamiliar pitched voice. "Did you know there's a type of sloth called ai? Well, they don't exist anymore, but apparently, they have very piercing cries." A man in his forties regards me from his chair. An uncommon sight, to see someone so alert.

Wushui snorts without looking up.

The sloth man looks at me with intrigue.

"Watch it, boy," Wushui, not missing the predator beat, hisses. "You ain't no regular. I can kick you out if I want to." He reminds me of my father and his "no-nonsense" manner.

The man looks outside, the rain still pouring heavily, tsks, then swerves his chair back to his screen.

Hermes leans over, the leather of her chair creaking, with fingers paused, hovering over the e-glass with a clear stylus in front of her. She's halfway completed a comic panel for an advertisement selling AWAKE pills. I peek at the logo in the corner—a small company I've been writing for as well. The perk of this job is the pills they send us every month. They're useful, but over time, my body seems to be getting too used to them for them to have the same initial impact.

"Don't worry about him. I see this jerk hanging around where I live sometimes, but the aunties and uncles upstairs always chase him away. Waiting for an ex, or something."

I'm not worried, but it's better to err on the side of caution around people with obsessive behaviour like that. At least behaviours that concern other people rather than a simple personal habit or tick. I can sympathize with the man. But it's not a kind of desperation I want to feel. It would only deter me from work, and the missing hours would prove to be far more painful than heartache in the long run when my

Coin account drains faster than the decreasing debt.

"Been stalking her socials here. He might slink around to your end too. Watch out." Hermes shakes her head, hand flying once more over the comic panels.

I glance again at the man and then at his screen. On the screen is the image of a woman in her thirties with a gentle smile.

Mother used to hang around her ex-girlfriend's workplace before New Era, before her marriage to Father. She did nothing. Just waited until her ex finished work and left before the woman came out. Mother used to pick her up every day the same way before they broke up.

Maybe it was the familiarity of the action she couldn't let go of, rather than the person. Or maybe it was both. She did the same thing with Father when they started dating. Perhaps it was the same for this man. But after starting at New Era, nothing outside of work mattered.

I suppose it can be a good thing to not be able to feel, to so single mindedly focus on accomplishing one thing and one thing only. It's simple, it's numbing, but it's also lifeless. And sometimes lifelessness is preferable.

"You found *the one* yet?" I tease as I wait for Wushui to unlock my e-glass screen. Hermes, though she might have not look like the typical romantic—with her beanie pulled over her brows and ears, and round glasses hovering at the tip of her nose—is one for idealistic dreams of perfect relationships—or used to be.

"Stop it," Hermes says, waving a dismissive hand. But her expression wilts, and I regret asking, even as a joke. "We both know we don't have the time for that. No human or any other species can shackle these fingers."

She wiggles her digits and draws a smile from me.

I tap my fingers erratically, looking to Wushui, who is taking more time than usual today. There are still five minutes left before I start work, but I'm antsy. I try not to log in early, to snuff my nerves, so I don't end up coming earlier and earlier until I'm here twenty-four hours a day like Wushui.

I should be used to the settled routine by now, having worked as an AI writer for the past five years. But the breaking of a cold sweat, the jittering hands, the staccato heartbeats when I'm facing deadlines never cease. I suppose that makes me more meticulous and efficient about my work, and ensures I keep clients, but it isn't great for long-term health, though lacking food is not much better.

My work hours have already increased from ten hours to eleven and a half. I can't remember the last time I had a proper break. It's still better than working for New Era with their fifteen-hour workdays, stuck within those suffocating skyscrapers. Sure, it's comfortable and they pay for housing outside of the New Era buildings if the workers so choose, but with that many hours, it's unlikely they get to spend much time outside work anyway. It's only an empty incentive for those who don't yet know what it's like to work for the monopoly.

I pick up the headphones settled just beneath the e-glass, then wrap the soft cushion around my ears. The rest of the world mutes. Tunnel vision is how Wushui describes my working state, much like everyone else's. Unlike Hermes, who frequently takes off her headphones to make conversation, I don't have the luxury of having those fleeting minutes.

One thing I love about Mao Tou Ying, though, is how meticulous Wushui is about hiding what goes on in each of the thirty or so systems in the cafe. But that means frequent government check-ins, which always sets me back an hour or two. From what I know, Wushui's record is still clean. Or if it isn't, maybe he slid money under the table to keep the officials quiet. Where the money comes from, I don't have a clue. He charges me and Hermes barely anything to use the e-glass screens, but I have a feeling not everyone here is being charged the same. For those who can afford more, he might charge more. Or so I assume.

The app I code launches on the e-glass. The title drifts across the screen as it boots up: *I AM AI.*

It isn't a lie. I am Ai, though not necessarily an actual AI. But marketing myself as an actual AI seems to bring in more clients and won't draw as much attention from New Era.

The main screen displays my one hundred twenty-three clients at a bar on the left side and the deadlines for writing projects I'd picked up and have yet to finish, along with a pending list of new projects waiting for confirmation. I scroll through the nudges for copywriting, a few advertisements and speeches, along with research documents and other ghostwriting assignments.

When I took on my first ghostwriting client, I felt like a fraud, like those people who say they're fluent in a language in which they are brokenly conversational at best. But it is better to be hired, even if I end up writing advertisements, research papers, or legal documents removed from my focus in fiction. Time waits for no one, and neither does Emit.

Wait—

I pull up the ping notifications that consist of deadlines for written work. My fingers fly over the holokeys, each letter flickering with each tap. The maximum number of desktops I can have active at once is fifty, but there isn't a limit to the number of documents and web tabs. Each desktop has a handful of documents and so many open tabs that there is an infinity symbol rather than the actual number of pages.

After scheduling a few new projects and the required research—some fiction and nonfiction pieces based on events like the rise of New Era, the fall of the forests of Feng, the life of Roaches— I take note of any last-minute projects with end-of-the-day deadlines.

A new request pops up just as I'm about to start on the nonfiction piece that glorifies New Era. I don't want to write it, but at least I have control over the words that go on the page. At times, I might sneak in snide comments that are usually missed unless someone looks closely enough. More often than not, only the protestors will pick up these interpretations.

150,000-word research paper on the benefits of AI writing and art—Deadline: by the end of tomorrow.

I almost chuckle at the irony. Even if I'm desperate, I have enough sense to pass on the job—

both because it's impossible, but also because it would be unethical, given my identity as a writer and my friendship with Hermes. I hover my finger above the decline button but catch sight of the completion bonus: one hundred fifty thousand Coin. My eye twitches. That will cover more than half of the debt I have remaining. I pick at the skin around my fingers, rub the back of my neck, feel the rash already building there. I rip a little too much away from the corner of my nail, and a bead of blood falls onto the table. There will be too much research necessary, and I will be pulling my hair out trying to write what I don't believe in. It will be much easier if this job popped up after my appointment with Joan, when my heart, the pulsing, chasing, reminder of humanity and its stress, anxiety, imperfection, is gone.

I press "accept."

I quickly finish a story for an interactive fiction website looking for more content and instantly receive a new review on their appreciation of my "different style" compared to other AI programs they source from. No client questions it since the subscription is only ten Coin a month, rather than the usual fifty Coin for New Era AI's fully automated service.

Then I start on the beast of an article.

"Ai." I turn to see Hermes with her attention fixed on a pop-up window of the e-application store. There is a new app that is basically a rip-off of my own: *I AM A.I.* There's not much of a difference in the name except for the clarification of the abbreviation. The subscription is eight Coin a month.

I can't help but think it's New Era's way of shutting me down. It isn't the first time the company has resorted to such tactics. As soon as my app falls, this new replica will also disappear.

Another ping.

A client seems to have discovered the new service and has unsubscribed—in the explanation box, they hide nothing in their reasoning: *New cheaper app*. But I can't go any lower than ten Coin. I might get away with nine Coin. Even that might be stretching it. The new app doesn't have many ratings or reviews, so I can only hope it will fail like many other apps after not getting enough traffic. The New Era AI app dominates most of the market, even with its prohibitive cost, snuffing out competition once it threatens to take close to 0.5% of their customer base.

It's difficult for Independents to survive. The only appeal I have is the illusion of demand and "uniqueness" I created by accepting a limited number of clients in comparison to any other app that attempts to compete with New Era. Anyone new to my app will have to apply and be put on the waiting list, which makes it seem as though my program is one highly sought after and in demand, while not taking enough customers from New Era to raise any concern.

I can send out an ad and increase my list limit from a hundred thirty to a hundred fifty clients, but that means even longer hours, less sleep, and further limiting snacks to save money. Sometimes I go into what Hermes calls "hyperfocus mode"—when I forget I'm human entirely as I remain glued to my seat, the only things moving are my fingers and the tracking flicks of my eyes across the screen.

I don't have enough saved for another upgrade, and my credit score is less than ideal given my parents' and my aunt's combined debt, but the mechanic I usually visit is kind, or at least kind enough to let me put things on the tab and slowly pay it off without interest. They remind me of my aunt who passed too early. I lived with her until I was eighteen and moved out, but I didn't know her debt would be added on top of my parents', until one day I received the letter from New Era. I should have guessed. She had no children of her own.

But it was the price she had to pay for refusing

to keep up with the rapidly developing tech and the shifting culture and job markets that came with it. She used to be a manual laborer, but during the Annual Layoff, she was unlucky enough to be let go. By then, it was too late to even become a Roach. Landfills are few now, and Roaches roam the streets, picking up anything they can. I'd thought about applying to become a Roach once, until I saw my aunt huddled by the trash, staring at what would be her dinner after she handed me what was left of the freeze-dried fruit at the back of her nearly empty cupboards.

With the government passing the "No Trash" law soon, it will be difficult for Roaches to find food to survive, much less afford any "real" food. To pick up any tech-based jobs with so many children who are much faster at grasping the new tech would be difficult as well—and those under eighteen weren't paid as much. *It isn't child labour*, they say. *We're offering them learning opportunities —experience.*

The problem is, even the teens who perform more efficiently and produce greater quality work than some adults *still* received only half their mature counterparts' salaries.

I turn back to the one hundred fifty thousand-word article, physically feeling the time ticking away with each second I spend thinking, constructing each sentence. My typing speed increases, but I can feel the quality of my work decreasing, the anxiety already thundering within me growing, my breaths becoming shallow as I hit the first ten thousand-word mark. Typos and inconsistencies litter the document, and more than once I think of using an AI program to help me fix the mess I created.

But I don't.

I continue on my own.

A TAP on my arm shakes my attention. I check the time, and though it only feels like seconds, it's already been hours. I can't remember what it's like not to look at lines of text and blocks of colour, all of it mixing together with the foggy background of Mao Tou Ying.

"What?" I shout.

Hermes flinches.

I snap my mouth shut, ducking my head in an instant, and mumble, "Sorry."

Hermes sighs. "In case I don't catch you when you leave," she says with a slight frown.

It's been four hours since I arrived. I nod without meeting her eyes. She's made a habit of telling me when she's going to work on her current paintings in the booth at the back. An unnecessary gesture, really, but I still appreciate it. I wonder how far along she is on her current piece and if it's a commission for New Era, a wealthy collector, or might I see it back at the honeycomb?

I hope she is working on a piece for joy rather than a contracted one, but I also know she has little extra time for such flexible and artistic exploration, even as her commissioners insist she has creative freedom and expression. But Hermes knows their true intentions, and though she always complains about the conflicting interests, she signs contract after contract anyhow.

They don't actually want us. They just want us to produce what they are looking for, exactly as they want it—not much different from AI, but they can slap our names on it to sway the AI protestors. "Look we're hiring human artists and writers!" they'll say. But nothing about what we make for them will seem human—only manipulated creations. We both know New Era only comes up with these campaigns to settle down protestors. *Their contracts are only temporary, project-based contracts*, Hermes insists.

I'm not sure who she is trying to convince that she still holds some sliver of power—me, New Era, or only a hopeful illusion she offers herself as justification for the soulless things she has been producing recently for the monopoly?

New Era and death might as well be one entity with the control they have over people's lives and the futile hope that escape might ever be possible once anyone signs their life away. I would rather die under the bridge than to pass, seen as a simple pawn, in New Era's easy path to dominance, even if they try to make it seem like the most glorious thing. Even if I'm being paid little for struggling Independents, anything is better than working for New Era, or even like Hermes, being under a "flexible contract." The contracts, the promises, all mean nothing, really. They will toss her like they do everyone else as soon as she ceases to be useful, especially as she gains too much attention and support from the public, as soon as the protestors are rioting for the liberation of her true art. Maybe there is a chance for unrestricted, "true art" again, but I have trouble picturing such a world—at least when it comes to Emit.

My eyes remain unflinching from my screen. The time between each blink lengthens. Maybe I'll need eye replacements soon. I'm sixty thousand words in, but the whole day is already almost gone. I'll return home quickly tonight so the neighbours will have power and return to Mao Tou Ying early tomorrow.

Hermes shuts down her e-glass and shakes

her head. "Take care of yourself, okay?" she says, then points at the USB dangling by my arm. "And don't forget to charge before you leave."

I scramble to flick off the dust guard in the middle of my forearm and insert the USB into the port. The cord must have pulled loose when I shifted in my seat earlier. I'd gone into power-saving mode without notice—I'd turned off the warning function of my watch months ago. 5%.

The small lightning bolt icon appears on the screen and glows in neon teal under the skin on my forearm. Relief cools the sweat on my back.

Sweat pools above my lip and drips down the side of my forehead. There are always a thousand different thoughts, each going in a thousand different directions—all centered around work and the number of things I have yet to cross out on my to-do lists. I want to put them in boxes, store them until they're needed, but this level of brain upgrade isn't yet available, at least not for what I can afford.

"Ai-ya—!"

Without looking, I swat where I assume Auntie Narwani is hovering near my port. My hand meets air.

I pry my eyes open and sit up when I remember I still have ninety thousand words remaining to write. In a scramble, I almost bump into Auntie Narwani by the entrance of my small box unit. She's pinching her features together while glaring out the window. A wire trails from my arm, but nothing is attached to it. Just outside, sitting on one step, is Nemo, flying her drone.

"Stop it. Stop this at once! You've been playing with that thing for hours!" Auntie Narwani waves her arm around.

Hours?

I quickly check my watch. I slept through my alarm, but not just that—

5%.

As much as I want to shout at Nemo, this mistake is my own. I should lock my unit, take my key back from Auntie Narwani. I've been too careless.

Outside, clouds collect in the distance, moving forth like an ominous, opaque grey mass towards the sun hanging above us, already dimmed by fog, waiting, wanting to consume the glowing celestial being, snuff it out, rip out of our hands the few minutes of nutrients we might squeeze from the waning light that is already barely present, to drink in the vitamin D we all lack. Maybe evolution will be kind and wipe it from our systems of need. Or eventually, we can ask a mechanic to get rid of it.

I imagine stepping coatless into the storm, face and palms upturned.

I would become a spasming mass, not human, not robot, and certainly not AI, but just Ai, laying in a puddle. No one in Emit will bat their eyes twice before stepping over, around, or on me in the passing. Because all these people either want to become AIs too, have an AI of their own, or want nothing to do with them, but are stuck tolerating the existence of such rapidly advancing technology because the new generations are reliant on it; the "solutions" are reliant on it. The innovators cradle their creations like children, saying they will change the world, they will better our lives, they will—

I rush out, hoping to reach Mao Tou Ying before it's too late.

As I scale up the ladder, my battery drops to 4%.

Mao Tou Ying is still too far.

Mao Tou Ying's winking lights are up ahead.

I trudge my way through the rain and buzz when I reach the entrance.

1%.

Wushui takes his time today, but instead of waiting patiently, I pound hard at the door.

"Wushui," I yell.

Please.

No answer.

I draw in a shuddering breath. "Wu—!"

The door unlocks, and I tumble in, splashing mud and water everywhere, much to Niao's protest. But I don't have time to care. Without changing into the slippers, I run towards Hermes' e-glass, because mine has yet to be unlocked, and plunge the cord into her system and then plug it into my port.

A sigh of relief escapes me, but everyone is watching me like I have a second head.

"Should get yourself checked. At the doctors, or whatever," Wushui says, not mentioning the slippers, and unlocks my e-glass screen. He knows none of us can afford doctors, not when we live on this side of the bridge, anyhow. Besides, a human doctor is unlikely to be helpful to me at this point.

I nod but say nothing and take off my dripping boots. There is no saving the carpet, and Wushui knows I won't be able to afford the cleaning fee. I'll work overtime the next couple of days, maybe bump my client limit to a hundred sixty to make up for the mess. I can use some of the one hundred fifty thousand Coin bonus too—if I finish the article.

I will finish.

Wushui's expression then smooths out, and he shrugs in response. His nonchalance, though some may find rude, is comforting to me, because it is also a validation that I'm okay, that I will live the night, that it's not so worrisome to leave his sight. I smile at the thought. I am still okay. I'm only missing two hours. I can work faster to make it up.

"I'm sorry," I mutter at the bewildered Hermes and notice how often I've been apologizing.

She snaps out of her shock and raises her hands in surrender. "No, no. Don't worry about it."

Without another word, I turn, settle myself in my seat and re-plug myself into my e-glass, and log onto *I AM AI*. Hermes stares at me without another word before heading to her booth. I envy the luxury she has, no matter how little, to work on the kind of art she believes in.

After half an hour, I'm hovering at just above 5%, charging slower than usual. The problem should be fixed after my appointment with Joan. . . tonight. My appointment would be just before the article deadline. I think about rescheduling, but it's better to just push through and finish the article.

I'm nearing one hundred thousand words total after adding forty thousand to the sixty thousand I had the day before when my e-glass shuts off. But not just my e-glass, Mao Tou Ying itself goes dark. A series of groans echo around the room, and among the sounds is my huff of frustration.

"Don't worry, don't worry. The power should be back on in no time!" Niao calls as people leave without paying.

The frown on Wushui's face deepens.

An alert on my watch warns me about my low battery.

I minimize the health screen and start working from my watch, the screen only the size of two palms together. Typing with one hand will drastically decrease my work speed, but I can't wait until the power comes back on.

I check the new *I AM A.I.* app and notice the ratings have been increasing at an alarming rate, likely given its low cost and unlimited client intake. I switch back to the article, my whole body now stooped towards the small holographic screen projecting from my watch.

"You need to eat, rest, sleep, go outside. You're not a robot," comes Wushui's voice. He has never shown concern before.

I wanted to tell him he doesn't know just how much of myself I have given up to circuitry, electricity, inhumanity, to gain even fleeting immortality and god-like efficiency, abilities that humans cannot and should not have, and would likely die trying to have.

"I know," I lie.

After half an hour, the power still doesn't come back on.

Hermes has returned from her booth while the other booth occupants stare blankly at the wall at the unlit e-glass screens. She looks unconcerned, and sits with her legs crossed in her chair, meditating. Many other customers already left, likely searching for another internet cafe that hopefully has power—something I probably should have done, but I never go into the city if I can help it. It's too close to New Era.

The emergency alert on my watch blinks, screams, begs me to pay attention, but I click "dismiss" again and again.

Today, I made another mistake in thinking I

can rely on Mao Tou Ying. But we are at the edge of a city that never blinks, and I never imagined that today would be the day that it closes its eyes. It seems too perfect, too timed for my demise. Surely the officials of Emit are fixing it, rapidly trying to find the issue because the elites and techies, and most importantly, New Era, will be unamused by this inconvenience in their lives, one that for me means life or death.

I prod at my circuit veins with their neon aqua lights slowly waning, noticeable only by me. My "blood" is draining right before my eyes.

I'm down to 1% again, and I've got five minutes tops, maybe six, if I allow my mind to go blank, my regenerative breaths to calm.

But I can't.

I continue working on the article, now at close to one hundred ten thousand words total and attempt to calm the panic from fogging my mind. More notifications and messages pop up for new projects and upcoming deadlines I've been putting off for this project alone. My looming expiry isn't as terrifying as not completing the article. I know I'll be losing some clients from pushing back their deadlines, but it will be worth it. But if I die, I guess it won't matter. It won't matter, it won't matter, it won't—

I AM AI

My eyes open, slow, and the light in Mao Tou Ying is back on—and so am I.

I look down at the USB plug dangling from my arm. It isn't mine, but one that's much longer, trailing towards a large bulky machine.

Wushui, cigar clutched between cracked lips, grunts. "Got the backup generator going. Forgot we had the thing." That is surely a lie. He wouldn't have pulled out the generator if I remained conscious. "You looked," he frowns, "like you were running low, real low."

For a second, I think he will be cliché and say I look pale, but I know that isn't possible, at least not anymore. I'm grateful that he saved me when he didn't have to. It wouldn't be the first time someone passed in his café, and it wouldn't be the first time he allowed it to happen. *Caring*, he'd always mused, *is a weakness*. But look at him now.

"Thank—"

He shakes his head. "You know we don't say that around here."

I nod, picking myself up, checking my battery. 50%.

Then the anxiety returns when I realize how long I've been out. The article.

"I am AI," I whisper the silly mantra I've used

since creating the app, to remind me of both who I am and who I need to be, even when those two things are nothing alike—a human, and something mechanic.

I open *I AM AI.*

Wushui snorts a laugh and smiles—something I rarely see outside of his frown.

Usually I would roll my eyes, offer a sheepish expression, maybe even return the smile, but today, I don't, and Wushui senses the shift in mood.

I pull open my watch, and my hope falls.

Over half my customers cancelled their subscriptions while I was unconscious, leaving poor reviews saying that the app is faulty, that they missed deadlines because of it.

Another ping. A message from Joan to remind me about my check-up. There is only five minutes left until the appointment, but the walk takes fifteen. There is no time left to finish the article, so after a few ragged breaths, I press "Withdraw" on the screen. With the replacement, at least I'll be able to earn back the customers.

Outside Mao Tou Ying, I resist the urge to drive myself against the brick wall and hurry down the street, dodging the dark alley and the muggers who often lurk there.

And with each passing second, the number of clients displayed on my watch decreases, and I don't know how to stop it. I blank. My breath quickens, and I want nothing more than to rip the watch from my arm, run from it all, much like how I ran from my parents' bodies when New Era brought them out of the tower. Avoidance is something I always turn to in times of extreme stress.

JOAN'S SHOP is located under a popular karaoke bar. Half of it is shared with a black-market tech supply dealer nicknamed The Scythe.

By the time I reach Joan's door, I'm drained.

I remove a loose brick from the wall and punch in the access code on the keypad hidden behind it while nursing my growing headache. My joints cry from the rain, from being unshielded.

"Hey! You're late," comes Joan's voice.

"Only by a minute," I say, shivering. Anticipation chews at my still human heart.

"Yeah, yeah. You know, I always say to come five minutes early." A sniff. "Did you snooze the notifications again?"

They already know the answer, but I know they're asking as a sneaky chiding.

The door unlocks and slides open, revealing

Joan in a wife-beater, muscles larger than I remember them to be. A few new tattoos battle for attention. They push a lock of hair from their eyes and step to the side. Joan's long bob has grown out slightly.

"After you," they say with a mocking sweep of their arm.

On my way down the dark hallway lit only by a dim neon pink glow, I eye the door that has a pen and ink scythe where the nameplate is. The door is left slightly ajar, and inside I see The Scythe, who codes my system upgrades, dressed in all black, hood up, in front of several e-glasses mounted on the wall.

In Joan's shop, everything is cast in shadow —shelves, cabinets, storage boxes—except for the single long metal table in the middle of the room. Dangling above the table is a low hanging lightbulb. If someone else is to work here, someone more human, I'd be concerned about how much they can see with this lighting, but knowing Joan, they already had eye enhancements implanted ages ago that are so advanced no one would be able to tell they aren't real.

I settle myself on top of Joan's table, the cold seeping through my damp joggers, biting into what remains of my blotchy human flesh. My fin-

I AM AI

gers twitch, itching to scratch at the growing rashes.

Joan plugs into my port. When my health stats appear on their e-glass screen, they make a noise between a scoff and an exasperated sigh.

"You really have a death wish, don't you?" Joan says and shakes their head before crossing their arms. One of the new tattoos is a snake with its fangs clamping down on its own body, the teeth piercing its own scaled armour.

I press my lips together, resisting the urge to say yes.

"And why are the health notifications off?" Joan asks, frowning when they check my e-watch that doubles as a health monitor and a work notification system.

I'd turned it off on purpose, so it wouldn't bother me during work. But I don't say this, and instead I say, "Must have accidentally tapped it while looking through notifications."

They look unconvinced but say nothing and know that scolding me would have little effect.

"Well," Joan says, "always double check, and keep the thing on, aight?"

I remain silent and hope they don't notice. They do.

Joan blows out a breath. "You'll wear yourself out at this rate, faster than I can fix you, maintain your parts, faster than you can make money to replace them. They're upping the costs, again, but you know that." Joan minimizes the page with my stats. "Electricity is supposed to get cheaper, not more expensive, but they do what they want." A humorless laugh.

For a moment, Joan looks thoughtful.

The cost, though worrying, is at the back of my mind in terms of priorities. I wake several times each night to check my notifications from existing and new clients, and in the morning, there is always a fog drifting in my mind. Exhaustion. Human exhaustion. It's becoming unsustainable.

"Awakeness," I begin, "can the new system fix it. Extend it? Make sleep unnecessary?"

Joan looks away, humming.

They seem undecided on voicing their thoughts. Then, without looking at me, they whisper, "Yes."

I've never been as conscious of the beating thing in my chest until this moment. Its pulse is often only a murmur, and now it's groaning its complaints. I'm both glad and terrified that such drastic procedures, which would have resulted in several months of recovery time for our ancestors, now only takes minutes.

I pick at my nails, chipped crescents unmaintained, then my eyes meet Joan's.

I'M STARING at my heart, sealed, preserved, which Joan will soon be shipping off to the buyer, and I wish I could hold it in my hand one last time.

I don't realize how silent my body feels until I wait for the steady beat, the rush of blood in my ears, only to meet the almost inaudible hum of the new electric currents running through me.

In my heart's place sits a new battery.

"You might regret it if you got rid of it all," Joan says when I reach the door. I wonder just how much of Joan is still human.

Outside, I turn off the health alerts again but keep the client notifications on, checking them every few seconds as I head back home.

I scroll through the unopened notifications and notice one from a client who was too impatient to wait for a response before cancelling their subscription. The usual panic and stress don't come. I stare at the number with nothing but numbness. I send out an ad and increase my client limit to two hundred.

THAT NIGHT AFTER MY PROCEDURE, upon returning to the honeycomb, my eyes linger on the red and orange of the emergency generators that make Emit appear as though in flames.

I RIP my arm away from a troubled Aunt Narwani without a second glance and don't pet Nemo on the head on my way out when she rushes over to me with her drone. The child follows for a few steps with disappointment and shock, but I pay her no mind as I make my way onto the top of the bridge. I know I should feel something, but I don't—at least not where the hollow left by my empty heart sits, but my brain still nags, though only for a moment before going quiet. Rather than scattered thoughts, they are now trained on a single goal: paying off the debt and leaving the bridge.

When I arrive at Mao Tou Ying, I bat away Niao's attempts at passing me water and snacks and stride barefoot to the e-glass screen I normally use. Wushui looks up, brows drawn low as I wait for him to boot the system. Rather than my normal impatience, I sit erect with my hands poised, waiting, eyes unwavering from the screen. I'm still ten minutes early.

Wushui unlocks the screen. My finger already hovers where my app is usually located, and I fly through tasks faster than usual. I find it much easier to ignore Hermes' small talk, much to her dismay. But when I see the new request for a one hundred eighty thousand-word book due tomorrow night, I pause. The bonus isn't nearly anything like the article I missed out on—one thousand Coin—but it's almost equivalent to what I make in a month. My brain calculates how long it might take me to finish it. If I stay overnight, I'll be able to complete it along with all the other tasks I have lined up for today. I press accept.

"Hey—"

"I'm busy," I say and increase the muting function level on my headphones.

Hermes plucks the headphones from my ears. "Can we talk?" Concern drags at all her features.

"I'll be working overnight," I say.

She pauses for a moment, glancing to the side at Niao and Wushui who are watching from the corner of their eyes, trying to not be obvious, but appearing much more apparent than if they had openly stared.

Finally, she says, "I can wait."

I nod, once, sharp, and take the headphones back.

It's already 4:00 p.m., and I'm still half an hour behind the estimated completion time I need for this document. I call Joan, who picks up after several wait tones, sounding groggy as though they had just taken a nap. I don't envy them. With the lack of a heart and new battery, my energy levels are much higher than before.

"How much will it take for a brain implant?" I ask without greeting.

Silence. "Steep. Very steep," Joan says, slow, hesitant.

"I can pay for it," I say. "Secure the new system for me before next week."

A grunt.

I hang up before I hear the answer.

AFTER THE CALL, Hermes spends the rest of her time staring at me. Though I don't feel discomfort from her actions, my brain urges me to stop her display of silent annoyance.

"What is it?" I ask.

"What happened at Joan's yesterday?"

"I got rid of my heart."

"You—"

"I'm also getting a new brain implant soon."

She falls silent and stares a hole into the left

side of my chest, then her gaze shifts to my forehead. I turn back to my work.

"I want to show you something," she says, tapping her pen against the desk in front of her.

"I don't have time."

"It's a gift," she tries.

"I don't want it."

Instead of getting offended, she drags me up from my seat and pulls me to her blacked out booth in the back. She rips the door open and shoves me in. Behind us, Niao and Wushui continue to watch. I have never been in Hermes' workspace before.

On the ground are scattered newspapers covered in paint. The e-glass has been uninstalled from this booth, and in its place is a narrow wall-to-wall desk with bottles of paints; palettes; cups of murky, multicoloured water; and brushes. Settled on an easel on the wall opposite the entrance is a painting as wide as I am tall, but its height only half my own.

Hermes gestures to the painting. It's the honeycomb with all our neighbours both inside and outside the square units turned hexagonal. Each of our painted faces are attached to the bodies of honeybees. Niao and Wushui hover in the distance in front of Mao Tou Ying, which Hermes had brought to life as a building-sized barn owl.

The owl has its wings spread, covering a large portion of Emit. Blue peaks from beneath the streaks of red and orange sky that resemble the city lit with its emergency lights. It seems Hermes had brushed on the new colour recently.

"Even though it seems like we have nothing, we have everything we need right here." She points to the honeycombs before dropping her hand. "It might be hard, but being together, working together, even if we're struggling. . . I don't know. There's something warming about it all, isn't there? I feel content somehow. Even with knowing that New Era might tear it all down someday."

I walk closer to the painting. I'm painted within my unit, bickering with Auntie Narwani and Nemo.

"I want to enjoy it while I can, you know? Being human, being together. . . or something like that," Hermes murmurs with a fond and thoughtful smile.

I try to recall both the joy and frustration but realize I can't. I say nothing and return to my desk. Hermes watches me from behind.

A notification pings from the client running the interaction fiction website. They have been with me long-term, ever since the second year of my app launching.

Reason for unsubscribing: The piece sounds like every other AI generated story. It doesn't have its usual emotion and humanity. Might as well go with another app if that's the case.

Several similar notifications arrive, commenting on the work I turned in earlier. Yet new customers quickly take the places of unsubscribers—clients who are looking for exactly what my work has come to resemble: cheap AI productions. I think of Auntie Narwani's clock, and the story she insists it holds.

I turn off my e-glass, ignoring all the other incoming notifications, the increasing and decreasing client counter, the reviews of both praise and criticism, and leave Mao Tou Ying.

Tears roll down my cheeks, but I don't feel the pain that causes them, though my brain knows I should.

I ARRIVE BACK at my unit just before 5:00 p.m. and huddle on the bare mattress on the ground. I shiver involuntarily against the futon when it touches the small of my back, still made of human flesh. My heart no longer registers the cold, but my body reacts because of muscle memory alone. My Bluetooth reconnects to all my neighbours' units, and their lights flicker on, but my eyes flutter closed. It's not difficult to slow my breaths or blank my mind now, but for some reason, I wish it was.

Within ten minutes, I hear the creak of steps climbing up the stairs towards me before I wake to see who it is. But I don't need to guess, because the same people show up on my doorstep all the time. Though this time, I'm too drained and exhausted to be glad for visitors. I check my battery, and it's already 2% lower, even on standby mode. Someone has been using my battery outside of just the units' light upon my return.

"Ai! Ai!" It's Nemo. In place of my usual pang of annoyance, of wanting to disconnect my Bluetooth and drown everyone out, of desiring nothing else but silence, I feel nothing at all.

I sit up and plaster a smile on my face without knowing why. "Hey," I say.

Nemo tumbles in, followed by Auntie Narwani complaining about how dangerous these stairs are and how difficult it is to climb from unit to unit, especially given days of strong wind.

"So happy you're back early today! We finally have warm soup!"

Soup. I glance at the time. 5:15 p.m. And I finally understand why Auntie Narwani is so insistent about the clock every day. She must use it to remind herself to prepare and serve food to all the residents each day.

Auntie Narwani stumbles into the room, the bowl of soup in her hand sloshing slightly off the side. The liquid, a strange murky beige, sits in a dirty Styrofoam bowl. It isn't much, yet it's also more than enough, and I wish the thought would fill me with the warmth I've sold away.

Auntie Narwani ambles over and plops down next to me with Nemo and holds out the bowl. She doesn't ask why I'm home early, and neither does Nemo.

I take a sip. It's chicken broth. My stomach gurgles when the liquid sinks to its bottom, and a strange warmth bubbles within.

A tear drops into the soup. It's mine.

"It's okay," Auntie Narwani says, patting my back.

But it isn't.

"Thank you," I say.

"There is no need to thank family," she says, smiling.

One of her teeth has fallen out, making her seem closer to a hundred than seventy. Behind Auntie Narwani, people from the community gather outside their units, on the stair landings, shouting conversation across to one another: Mrs. Gem holds her newborn, a child who likely won't last the year, as many children don't unless they have New Era's support; Nemo has left us and is now sprinting from unit to unit, pausing periodically to wheeze, hands on knees—her asthma is getting worse. The sound of the electric drill goes off again—something else broken.

I look away from them all and shut out the sounds.

Rather than gratitude, it is the return of the pain I felt when I lost my parents that stirs within my mind. The phantom of a heart throbs and tugs. The warmth, the sense of community, though both beautiful things, always risk loss and hurt.

"Thank you," I croak, and it feels like a goodbye.

I set down my bowl of soup and leave the unit.

"Come back soon," Auntie Narwani calls out.

I call Joan.

AT NIGHT, we all sit by the waterline, staring at Emit with its blue eyes open once more.

In silence, my neighbours all manually disconnect from my battery, leaving only the glow of moonlight above us.

From the bridge, a shadow climbs down and makes their way towards us.

Hermes. She takes quick strides, firm and resolute, until she looms above me.

She snatches my wrist and connects her own watch to mine and initiates a Coin transfer.

"What—"

"I sold the painting. For your brain implant," she says, then offers a weak smile.

I pull away. "Why?"

"I figured it was unfair for me to impose my own ideals onto you," she says, fiddling with the ends of her hair, her fingers paint-tinted.

"I canceled the appointment. I'm trying to get my heart back," I say, slow.

Silence.

I lean back and toss my head up.

"I've been a fool, haven't I?" I say with a choked laugh.

Hermes flops down and leans against me, eyeing the port on my arm. She hums. "You always have been."

I snort at the snide comment.

A notification jolts me. Joan. I pull up the message.

Looks like it's much easier buying a heart than selling it.

I wonder who is giving up their heart, and I

mourn for their loss within. A tear rolls down my cheeks, and I feel both the pain and relief that causes it—a sharp shock followed by a full blossoming ache. Though it won't be my original heart, I'm glad it will be one that trembles.

Hermes and I share a melancholic smile.

In the distance, a new New Era advertisement glares from the top of their highest skyscraper.

"Your... painting," I say.

We stare at the digitized version of Hermes' honeycombs, the advertisement promising New Era buildings of a similar "unique" structure and concept, and the forthcoming announcement about job application submissions to work for their new "community". The New Era tower in the painting has been altered to look like there is a queen bee settled on top. *Like a hive, we must work as one! Join our family!*

Hermes shakes her head. "Even if they take it and make it into something it isn't, at least we know to us it will always hold its true meaning."

"Our story," I say.

Auntie Narwani mutters about New Era's villainy. I grin at her defiance, the way she continues to struggle against New Era simply by being herself. Something that we all are doing—what binds us together.

Auntie Narwani then looks over with a smile,

revealing the growing gaps from missing teeth. She lays the stuttering clock on my lap and points. "Maybe we are broken, but we might not always remain that way."

I look down at the clock to see a small solar panel installed—something New Era has made very difficult to get. The bent hands struggle, and the slight squeal of hidden gears continue to click, and though this is only an object, I can't help but feel it's more alive than I am.

For the first time, I'm grateful for the quiet of our home under the bridge; of our offline connections; of our eyes reflecting not the light of screens, but the dark of the natural waters, even as it often threatens to drown us during heavy storms; and the choking thought at the back of our minds of the alarming loom of floods with the continuously rising sea levels.

And for the first time, I realize the beauty of fragility, the value of ache—to be able to bleed, to be able to fear, to tick and struggle ticking: to be truly human.

ACKNOWLEDGMENTS_

To Alan, Nancy, and Erin, thank you for your amazing work editing *I AM AI*. It is through human mind and hands from which it has been created, and it is through human minds and hands from which it has been completed.

To my mother who laboured over the cover art with me, for going through draft after draft and finalizing such an amazing watercolour portrait which serves as the foundation of the cover, and to Alan again who did the typography and design—a very human collaboration that made the final product all the more meaningful.

To Katie and Odyssey Workshop director Jeanne, thank you for reading the earliest version of this chaos and offering gentle guidance.

To all my blurbers for their more than generous words about this novelette—it is always the greatest honour and pleasure to receive praise from fellow writers.

To the readers, reviewers, podcasters, interviewers, fellow writers, among others who have read and will read this novelette, I wish it will bring you joy, and I wish it will bring you hope. May it urge you to hold tight to your heart, even when it brings you sorrow.

Always, to my family and my spouse Focus for their unending support and encouragement, I could ask for nothing more.

Again, to you who is reading this, you are enough.

And finally, to all those who curse at their fragility, the way I often do myself, this is what makes us human, this is what makes us alive, and this is what makes us irreplaceable.

ABOUT THE AUTHOR_

Ai Jiang is a Chinese-Canadian writer, a Nebula Award finalist, and an immigrant from Fujian. She is a member of HWA, SFWA, and Codex. Her work can be found in F&SF, The Dark, Uncanny, among others. She is the recipient of Odyssey Workshop's 2022 Fresh Voices Scholarship and the author of *Linghun* and *I AM AI*.

Find her online: aijiang.ca

A NOTE FROM
SHORTWAVE PUBLISHING_

Thank you for reading *I AM AI*!

If you enjoyed it, please consider writing a review or telling a friend! Word-of-mouth helps readers find more titles they may enjoy and that, in turn, helps us continue to publish more titles like this.

OUR WEBSITE
shortwavepublishing.com

SOCIAL MEDIA
@ShortwaveBooks

EMAIL US
contact@shortwavepublishing.com

www.ingramcontent.com/pod-product-compliance
Ingram Content Group UK Ltd.
Pitfield, Milton Keynes, MK11 3LW, UK
UKHW021354280125
4330UKWH00048B/1420

9 781959 565093